#58   APR 2 8 2010

W9-BFG-944

There's Something There!

THREE BEDTIME CLASSICS

There's Something in My Attic

There's a Nightmare in My Closet

There's an Alligator Under My Bed

written and illustrated by MERCER MAYER

DIAL

DIAL BOOKS
A member of Penguin Group (USA) Inc.
Published by The Penguin Group
Penguin Group (USA) Inc., 375 Hudson Street, New York, NY 10014, U.S.A.

Penguin Group (Canada), 90 Eglinton Avenue East, Suite 700, Toronto, Ontario,
Canada M4P 2Y3 (a division of Pearson Penguin Canada Inc.)
Penguin Books Ltd, 80 Strand, London WC2R 0RL, England
Penguin Ireland, 25 St. Stephen's Green, Dublin 2, Ireland
(a division of Penguin Books Ltd)
Penguin Group (Australia), 250 Camberwell Road, Camberwell, Victoria 3124,
Australia (a division of Pearson Australia Group Pty Ltd)
Penguin Books India Pvt Ltd, 11 Community Centre, Panchsheel Park,
New Delhi – 110 017, India
Penguin Group (NZ), Cnr Airborne and Rosedale Roads, Albany, Auckland 1310,
New Zealand (a division of Pearson New Zealand Ltd)
Penguin Books (South Africa) (Pty) Ltd, 24 Sturdee Avenue, Rosebank,
Johannesburg 2196, South Africa
Penguin Books Ltd, Registered Offices: 80 Strand, London WC2R 0RL, England

There's a Nightmare in My Closet
Copyright © 1968 by Mercer Mayer

There's an Alligator Under My Bed
Copyright © 1987 by Mercer Mayer

There's Something in My Attic
Copyright © 1988 by Mercer Mayer

ISBN 0-8037-3133-7

This edition created exclusively for Barnes & Noble Inc., under
ISBN-13: 978-0-7607-7424-3
ISBN-10: 0-7607-7424-2

Printed and bound in Mexico.

3   5   7   9   10   8   6   4

THERE'S SOMETHING IN MY ATTIC

written and illustrated by MERCER MAYER

THERE'S SOMETHING
IN MY ATTIC

written and illustrated by MERCER MAYER

To Jessie, my daughter,
with love

Who was touched by Goopy
and went to Singapore?
Who had witches in the trees
and a finger on the door?
Who didn't like the thumber
or the lightning anymore?

I was never afraid of anything
when we lived in the city,
but now we live on a farm.

At night when the lights go out,
I get scared,

because I can hear

a nightmare in the attic

right above my head.

It doesn't seem to bother Mom and Dad.

They say it's probably mice.

But it sounds too big to be mice.

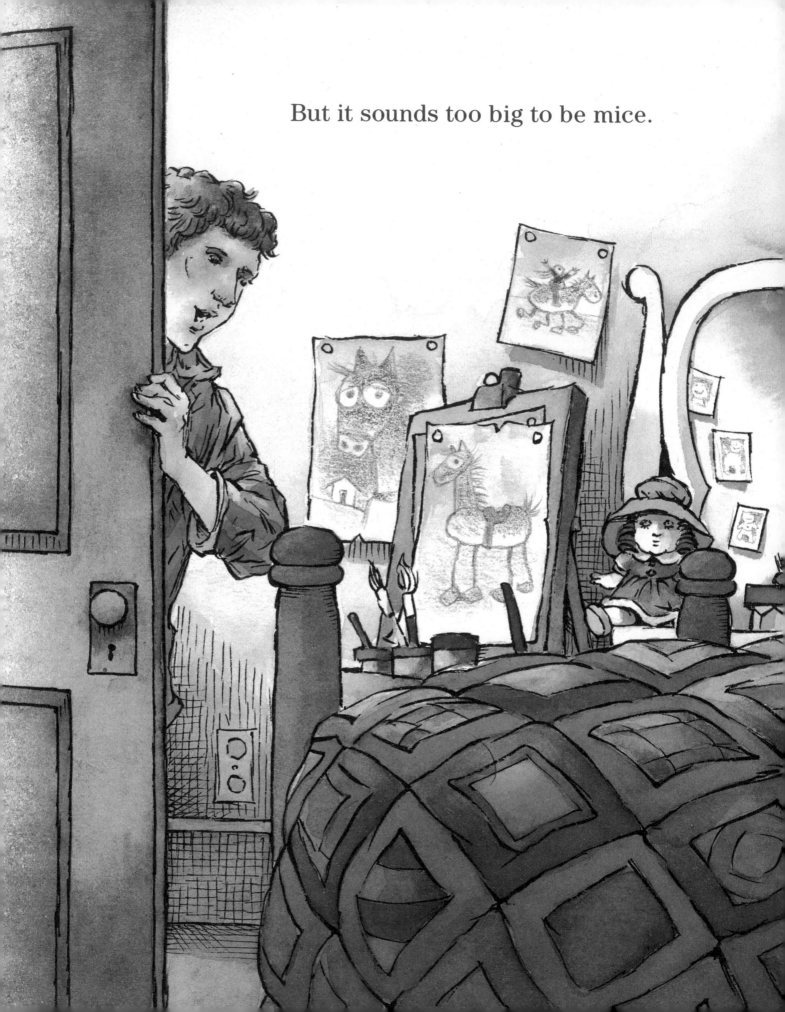

I decided to lasso that nightmare
and bring it down to show them.

I'd just be brave and sneak quietly
into the attic with my lasso ready.

It wasn't there.
But I noticed a bunch of toys
I thought were lost
lying in a pile behind some boxes.

Something weird was going on for sure.
Then I heard it creeping up the stairs.

There it was, standing in front of me
with my brand-new teddy bear
it had just stolen from my room.

"Hey," I called. "That's my teddy bear!
Give it to me!"
But the nightmare tried to sneak back
down the stairs.

So I chased it.

Then I lassoed it.

It was hugging my bear as hard as it could.

"Be careful, Nightmare," I said,
"or you'll rip my bear."

I tried to get my bear back,
but it wouldn't let go.

So I pulled it down the hall
to my parents' room.

I flipped on the lights

to show them the nightmare I captured.
I was sure they would be amazed.

But nightmares are very tricky, and
sometimes they just slip away.

I'll just have to get my bear back tomorrow.

THERE'S A NIGHTMARE
IN MY CLOSET

written and illustrated by MERCER MAYER

THERE'S A NIGHTMARE
IN MY CLOSET

written and illustrated by Mercer Mayer

Dial Books for Young Readers | *New York*

Marianna

From cotton to rabbit

There used to be a nightmare in my closet.

Before going to sleep,

I always closed the closet door.

I was even afraid to turn around and look.

When I was safe in bed, I'd peek...

sometimes.

One night I decided to get rid of my nightmare
once and for all.

As soon as the room was dark, I heard him creeping toward me.

Quickly I turned on the light and caught him sitting at the foot of my bed.

"Go away, Nightmare, or I'll shoot you," I said.

I shot him anyway.

My nightmare began to cry.

I was mad...

but not too mad.

"Nightmare, be quiet or you'll wake
Mommy and Daddy," I said.

He wouldn't stop crying so I took
him by the hand

and tucked him in bed

and closed the closet door.

I suppose there's another nightmare in my
closet, but my bed's not big enough for three.

THERE'S AN ALLIGATOR UNDER MY BED

written and illustrated by MERCER MAYER

THERE'S AN ALLIGATOR
UNDER MY BED

written and illustrated by MERCER MAYER

Dial Books for Young Readers / New York

To Alburn and Phillip

There used to be an alligator under my bed.

When it was time to go to sleep,
I had to be very careful

because I knew he was there.

But whenever I looked,
he hid...or something.

So I'd call Mom and Dad.

But they never saw it.

It was up to me.
I just had to do something
about that alligator.

So I went to the kitchen
to get some alligator bait.

I filled a paper bag full
of things alligators like to eat.

I put a peanut butter sandwich,
some fruit, and the last piece
of pie in the garage.

I put cookies down the hall.

I left fresh vegetables on the stairs.

I put a soda and some candy
next to my bed.
Then I watched and waited.

Sure enough, out he came
to get something to eat.

Then I hid in the hall closet.

I followed him down the stairs.

I followed him down the hall.

When he crawled into the garage,

I slammed the door and locked it.

Then I went to bed.
There wasn't even any mess to clean up.

Now that there is an alligator in the garage, I wonder if my dad will have any trouble getting in his car tomorrow morning.

I'll just leave him a note.